This book belongs to

_____

WISE
GRANDMA DUCK

WALT DISNEY FUN-TO-READ LIBRARY

A BANTAM BOOK
TORONTO • NEW YORK • LONDON • SYDNEY • AUCKLAND

Wise Grandma Duck   A Bantam Book/January 1986   All rights reserved.   Copyright © 1986 The Walt Disney Company.   This book may not be reproduced, in whole or in part, by mimeograph or any other means.

ISBN 0-553-05586-0

Published simultaneously in the United States and Canada.   Bantam Books are published by Bantam Books, Inc.   Its trademark, consisting of the words "Bantam Books" and the portrayal of a rooster, is Registered in U.S. Patent and Trademark Office and in other countries.   Marca Registrada.   Bantam Books, Inc., 666 Fifth Avenue, New York, New York 10103.   Printed in the United States of America   0 9 8 7 6 5

Huey looked out the car window. "There it is, Uncle Donald!" He could see Grandma Duck's farm at the end of the road. Louie and Dewey waved to a cow in the field.

"I can hardly wait to get there!" Donald said. "Fresh air, long naps, and Grandma's great food. What a vacation!"

Grandma was waiting at the gate. She
gave each of them a big hug and kiss.
"Come along, boys. Let's go up to the house
and get something to eat."

While they ate, Grandma Duck told them what was new on the farm. "My farmhand has gone. I have no one to do the chores anymore," she said.

"Don't worry, Grandma," said Louie.

"We can do them," said Huey and Dewey.

Donald did not say a word. Farm work was not his idea of a vacation.

The next morning the nephews were
ready for work.

"Let me see," said Grandma. "The
chicken house needs a good coat of paint."

Just then Donald came into the kitchen.
"My back hurts, Grandma. I can't work today."
"Oh, poor Donald," Grandma said. She
helped him out to the yard. "You just rest
here, dear, and I will bring you some
lemonade."

All day long Donald rested. He was
having a good time. When the dinner bell
rang, he jumped up and ran to the table.

"Boy, Uncle Donald, you got to the table fast," Louie said. "Your back must be feeling better."

Grandma Duck smiled. "And I'm glad. There is a lot of work to do tomorrow. The barn needs cleaning."

When Donald came downstairs the next morning, the nephews had already eaten breakfast. They were on their way to work.

"My stomach hurts," Donald groaned. "I don't think I can work today."

But Donald felt well enough to eat a great
big breakfast. Grandma sighed and shook
her head. Then she helped him up to bed.
    Alone in his room, Donald said to himself,
"Aaah! What a perfect way to spend the day."

Huey, Dewey, and Louie worked hard all day. They swept the barn floor. They brought fresh hay for the horse. They cleaned the windows.

In the evening they went up to Donald's room. "The work is all done, Uncle Donald," they said. "We worked together. It was fun."

"That's great!" said Donald. "And I feel much better. In fact, I'm so hungry I could eat everyone's supper!"

After supper, the boys rode the horse.

"Gee, that looks like fun. I think I'll try it," said Donald.

"I'm glad you are feeling better now, Donald. You can help the boys stack all that firewood tomorrow," said Grandma.

Donald looked. That heap of wood was as high as the barn!

The next morning there was something
else wrong with Donald.

"My arm hurts, Grandma," he said. "I
must have fallen out of bed. I guess I won't
be able to help stack that wood."

"Then what are you planning to do today?" Grandma asked.

"I'll watch the boys," said Donald. "I can tell them what they are doing wrong."

And that is just what Donald did. All
morning long he sat and watched. He sipped
cold drinks. And he gave a lot of orders.
Huey, Dewey, and Louie worked and worked.
At last, all the wood was in one neat pile.

That afternoon the boys decided to go
fishing. "Look at Uncle Donald," Huey
whispered. "His arm must be feeling better."

Sure enough, when Donald saw the
fishing poles, he wanted to go fishing too. "I
think my arm is better now, boys," he said.
"But you had better carry everything. I don't
want to hurt my arm again."
Grandma watched Donald go off with
the boys.

The next day, the apples were ready to be picked.

"You boys can eat as many apples as you want," Grandma said.

"Great!" cried Huey, Dewey, and Louie. They ran to the apple tree.

Grandma looked at Donald.

"My arm still hurts," he said. "I guess I'll just go sit under a tree and watch the boys again today. But I'll make sure they do a good job."

Huey, Dewey, and Louie loved to pick apples. Every hour they stopped to munch an apple or two—or three.

And Donald slept while the boys worked.

Then Grandma brought out a big tray of cookies. She put one in Donald's good hand. "Huey, throw your Uncle Donald an apple," she called.

Without thinking, Donald caught the apple with his sore arm.

Grandma smiled. "I'm glad your arm is better, Donald," she said.

When the boys were done, Grandma led them all to a hill. She put the empty cookie tray on the grass.

"It's time for some fun," she said. "Who wants to slide down the hill?"

"I do!" shouted Donald. Before the boys could move, Donald jumped on the tray. He slid down the hill.

For an hour they took turns sliding down the hill. Donald took more turns than anyone.

At last Grandma told them to go inside and rest. "You have two big jobs tomorrow," she said. "The corn and the pumpkins must be picked."

"<u>More</u> work?" Donald asked. He grabbed
the tray. "I'm going for one last ride," he
shouted. Then he slid down the hill very fast.

Donald slid faster and faster.
"Watch out, Uncle Donald!" shouted
Huey, Dewey, and Louie.

"Oh, Donald," cried Grandma.

Just as he was about to hit a tree, Donald jumped off. He rolled over and over on the grass.

Grandma and the boys ran down the hill.

"Ouch! My head!" moaned Donald.
Grandma looked for a bump. "I can't
seem to find anything wrong," she said.
"Well, my head hurts," said Donald with
a whine. "I had better go straight to bed."

"Poor Uncle Donald," said Louie. "I hope he is all right."

"I think he is just fine," Dewey said. "It's the thought of work that makes Uncle sick!"

The next morning Donald walked around with an ice bag on his head.

"Too bad Uncle Donald has a headache," Huey said. "This cornfield is a great place for hide-and-seek!"

Pumpkin picking was fun, too. When all the pumpkins were picked, Louie put Uncle Donald's hat on a pumpkin. Everyone laughed—except Donald.

That evening, Grandma told the boys that all the work was done. "No one works tomorrow except me," she said. "I am going to make a dinner of all the things you like best. That is my way of thanking you."

"Hurray!" shouted the nephews.

Donald pushed the ice bag off his head.

"My head feels better every minute," he said.

"By tomorrow I should be just fine."

"That's good, dear," said Grandma. "I wouldn't want you to miss our dinner."

The next day Grandma was busy in the
kitchen.

Huey, Dewey, and Louie kept busy too.
They brushed and combed Grandma's horse.
Soon it looked good enough to lead a parade.

Donald was busy trying to find out what Grandma was cooking.

"Run along, Donald. Don't be so nosy! I want this to be a real surprise," she said.

At last the dinner bell rang.

The nephews raced to the table, but Donald got there first.

Grandma put a big, covered plate in front of each boy.

One by one, Huey, Dewey, and Louie took the covers off their plates.

"It's corn on the cob!" Louie shouted.

"A whole apple pie!" said Huey.

"Pumpkin pie, my favorite!" cheered Dewey. "And with cream! Oh, boy!"

At last Grandma set the biggest plate of all in front of Donald.

Donald grabbed the cover from the plate. "But, but—" he sputtered.

"It's medicine!" said Louie. "It's for headaches, stomachaches, and sore muscles!"

Huey, Dewey, and Louie couldn't stop laughing.

"I hope you are happy, Donald, dear,"
Grandma said. "I wanted each of you to have
what you worked for."

Then she laughed, too. And for once in
his life, Donald Duck could not think of a
thing to say.